Molly's Magic

The Secret Pony

Molly's Magic

The Secret Pony

HOLLY WEBB

Illustrated by Erica Jane Waters

SCHOLASTIC

First published in the UK in 2009 by Scholastic Children's Books
An imprint of Scholastic Ltd
Euston House, 24 Eversholt Street
London, NW1 1DB, UK
Registered office: Westfield Road, Southam, Warwickshire, CV47 0RA
SCHOLASTIC and associated logos are trademarks and/or registered
trademarks of Scholastic Inc.

ISBN 978 1 407 10753 0

Printed by CPI Bookmarque, Croydon, CR0 4TD

1 3 5 7 9 10 8 6 4 2

www.scholastic.co.uk/zone

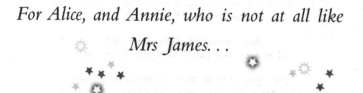

*For Alice, and Annie, who is not at all like
Mrs James. . .*

Chapter One

My Own Pony

Molly wandered down the lane, humming
to herself, and enjoying the bright autumn
sunshine. She stopped halfway along to
climb on the gate that led to the riding
school fields. Lots of the ponies were
turned out there this morning. Molly had
hoped they would be, and she'd raided
her mum's cupboard for sugar lumps.

Molly stood on the bottom rung of
the gate, which made her just the right
height to lean over the top and call to

1

the ponies, who were already looking up at her with interest. As soon as Molly held out her hand with a couple of sugar lumps, the two nearest ponies trotted over eagerly. She had ridden at the riding school a few times, and had often gone there with her dad, because he was their vet, so she knew these two ponies. The chestnut was called Bella, and the black pony was Treacle.

Molly stroked their noses, and fed them more sugar, and crooned compliments to them, but they didn't talk back. Of course, she didn't really expect them to, but Molly knew that some animals *could* talk, and she had met several who did. Sparkle the witch's kitten, Star and Stella the wish puppies, and just a week or so ago, Snowdrop, the cheeky vanishing rabbit.

When they'd finished up all the sugar, the ponies licked at her hands, and sniffed her pockets hopefully, just in case she had some more sugar or even mints hidden away, then trotted off to graze again.

Molly slid down from the gate, and walked on, thinking about ponies. She had looked after Snowdrop the rabbit for her owner, a magician called the Amazing Albert, while he was away. It had been a tricky job, because Snowdrop was extremely fussy, and she kept accidentally disappearing. But Molly's mum and dad had been really impressed with the way she'd looked after Snowdrop, and they'd said that very soon they'd think about letting Molly have a pet of her own.

Ever since then, Molly had been wondering about what sort of pet she should have. She hadn't really thought about a pony, but she did love to ride. She was quite good at it, and there was plenty of space round the old farmhouse where they lived. A pony of her very own! That would be wonderful. A couple of girls in her class at school had their own ponies, and Jess actually rode to school on hers. She lived a little way out of Larkfield, so she rode in and stabled her pony in a field near to the school.

Molly looked
at her watch
and speeded
up a bit. She'd
spent longer than
she'd realized
talking to Bella
and Treacle.
Grandad would
be expecting her
already. Molly
was heading for
the forge, where her grandad worked
as a blacksmith. It was only half a mile
down the lane from Larkfield Farm Vets,
so she was allowed to walk there on her
own sometimes. But if she was late, and
Grandad got worried and phoned Mum,
there would be a huge fuss.

Besides, she wanted to get to the forge.

Grandad had two horses booked in for shoeing today, and he'd asked Molly to come and help. Even before she had discovered her magical ability, Molly had always been very good at calming nervous animals, and Grandad liked her to hold the horses sometimes.

Usually on a Saturday, Molly would be helping her dad at the surgery, doing the same sort of thing, but Dad was busy with an urgent operation today. He'd even cancelled morning surgery, because a cat had been brought in late last night with very serious injuries after a car accident. This morning Dad was going to operate on the poor cat's leg. Molly nibbled her bottom lip. Dad was worried about the cat, she could tell. Molly had heard him telling Mum that he thought it might be too weak for the operation.

Molly sighed, hoping it was going all right back at the surgery, and ran the last little way down the lane to the forge. A very smart navy blue horsebox was standing outside, and Molly hurried in. The forge was round the back of Grandad's cottage, and a path led up into the yard. There was no sound of hammering, so Grandad hadn't started yet.

Suddenly there was a shrill whinny of fear, a noise that sent a shiver running through Molly's bones. What was going on? Molly had never heard a horse sound that scared, especially not anywhere near Grandad. He was known throughout the whole area as a good blacksmith. He was so gentle with the horses – Molly's mum said that Molly had inherited some of his gift.

She crept into the yard, not wanting to scare the horse any more, and peered over into the open forge.

Then she gasped. Standing in the dim forge, lit by the dancing gas flames, was the most beautiful pony she had ever seen.

Chapter Two

The Silver Pony

The silver-white pony was stamping and struggling and pulling at his lead-rope, obviously very scared. His long, white mane was tossing everywhere, and his big eyes were panicked.

"Oh, Molly!" Grandad sounded glad to see her. "Would you be able to help Mrs James hold Silver? He's a bit nervous."

Mrs James was a tall woman, with very dark hair, and a stern face. She looked at Molly's grandad in surprise, and seemed quite annoyed. "I really don't think a little girl is going to make much difference," she snapped.

Molly stared at her. She was so rude! And it wasn't as if she was managing the pony very well herself. The poor thing was terrified.

Grandad frowned. "Molly is very good at calming horses," he said, his voice polite, but firm.

Just then, the pony took advantage of them all being distracted, and tossed his head high, yanking the lead-rope out of Mrs James's hand.

Then he wheeled round, and backed up against the wall, putting his head down and pawing the ground, as though he was planning to shove his way through them and make a dash out of the forge.

Molly gasped, but not because she was frightened. As the pony ducked his head, just for a second in the firelight, Molly had seen a shining, pearly horn between his ears.

Silver wasn't a pony.

He was a unicorn!

"Horrible animal," Mrs James said angrily. "I don't know what's the matter with him."

Molly didn't dare say it, of course, but she had a feeling that belonging to Mrs James might be quite a lot of what was wrong with Silver. She would upset anyone.

Molly tried hard to remember everything she'd ever read about unicorns, but all she could think of was that their horns were very sharp, which wasn't helpful. Slowly, she took a step towards Silver, who was still pressed back against the wall of the forge, his sides heaving.

He eyed her uncertainly, twisting his head from side to side to see her better, and Molly saw the horn again. She definitely hadn't imagined it. She held out her hand, and gently stroked the side of his neck. He was trembling.

Silver drew a deep, shuddering breath, and nuzzled against Molly's shoulder. He stared into her eyes, and Molly noticed that his own eyes were blue. She had seen a blue-eyed pony once before, but Silver's eyes were a deep, dark blue, like the sea on a summer day. They were beautiful.

You know what I am... A soft, gentle voice spoke in her mind, and Molly nodded slightly. She had been wondering if he would talk to her.

"Well, lead him back over here, girl!" Mrs James snapped, and Silver flinched at her voice.

Molly turned and glared at Mrs James. She just stopped herself from being rude back — she didn't want Mrs James to be upset with Grandad. "In a minute," she said, forcing herself to be polite. "He's still very frightened."

I'm not!

I know, but I have to tell her something, Molly explained. It was very odd, talking without saying anything. She'd never been able to do it before, although she had heard Sparkle and Star's voices in her head. *Has she owned you for long?*

She doesn't own me. No one owns me. I was stolen from my home, and I need to find my way back. She wants to put shoes on me, Molly, and I can't let her! Iron shoes will make me just an ordinary pony, I won't be a unicorn any more. You have to help me. . .

I will, Molly promised. She turned back to Grandad and Mrs James. "I can get him to stand, but he won't let you shoe him," she told Grandad.

"What?" Mrs James sounded furious. "What nonsense! He told you that, did he?"

Molly wondered what Mrs James would say if she told her that yes, he had. But it probably wasn't a good idea. "He seems afraid of being shod," she said slowly. It was almost the truth.

"Well, he's never been shod before," Grandad said thoughtfully.

Mrs James stared at him. "Never been shod? Of course he has!"

"I promise you, he hasn't." Grandad came over to Molly and Silver, and gently stroked Silver's nose. Then he carefully lifted up one of Silver's hind feet.

"Look – no nail marks. He's never had shoes."

Mrs James was frowning angrily. "He was sold to me as a gentle riding pony, an ideal beginner's pony for my daughter!"

"Well, I'm afraid he certainly isn't that," Grandad said, looking at Silver's wild eyes, and his hoof that was nervously pawing the dusty stone floor.

"I shall demand my money back," Mrs James muttered.

"Why don't you try taking him to a specialist trainer?" Grandad suggested. "I can give you some people to call. I don't think he's been properly broken for riding, and he may have been mistreated, to be this scared."

"So you're not going to shoe him?" Mrs James demanded, her hands angrily on her hips.

Grandad stared back silently, and Mrs James shifted uncomfortably as he looked at her. "No, I'm not," he finally told her. "This pony is terrified, and I'm not going to risk damaging his spirit for ever. Until he's willing to be shod, I won't shoe him."

I like your grandfather... Silver told Molly.

17

Me too! Molly replied. She was very impressed with Grandad, especially as Mrs James would probably go and tell all her horsy friends mean things about him.

Mrs James took hold of Silver's lead-rope, and yanked him towards her, dragging him out of the forge.

Molly gasped, and made a move to stop her, but Silver shook his mane, the long silvery-white locks shaking sparkles all over the forge. *Don't worry. She won't keep me for long. I'll be back to find you, Molly. You will help me get home, won't you?*

Molly nodded fiercely. "I promise!" she whispered. She wanted to say it out loud. She looked up as Silver paced out of sight down the little lane to the horse-box, and found Grandad staring at her, puzzled.

"You know, Molly, I've the strangest feeling that that was no ordinary horse..."

Chapter Three

A Magical Morning

Molly dreamed of unicorns that night, and the next. They were galloping through forests, and leaping over rivers, their hooves leaving silvery trails in the darkness. Then she woke up on Monday morning convinced that someone was calling her. It wasn't properly light in her bedroom yet though. Was Mum really calling her this early? Molly rolled over and looked sleepily at her clock. Five o'clock in the morning! She must have imagined it. Just a dream, probably, she thought, and snuggled back into her duvet.

Molly!

Molly sat up. She definitely hadn't imagined *that*. She threw back her covers, and crept out of bed, shivering a little in the chilly autumn morning. She peeped out through her bedroom curtains, remembering Sparkle climbing up to

The Unicorn

PONY

her windowsill a few weeks ago, but no one was there.

The orchard, Molly!

Oh! Molly was starting to wake up properly now, and she recognized the voice in her mind. It was Silver, the unicorn – he'd found her at last. She had been worrying that he wouldn't know where she lived. Quickly she threw on her school uniform. That way she wouldn't have to get changed later, and if anyone asked why she was outside, she could just say that she'd woken up early and felt like a walk, although she wasn't sure how convinced Mum would be by that.

Then she tiptoed through the grey, early-morning house, grabbing her jacket and wellies and heading out to the orchard. It was a beautiful morning, cold, but with bright sunshine just starting to break through the swirls of mysterious mist.

Molly leaned on the orchard gate. It was such a magical time of day, with the mist trailing round the trees, and dewdrops on all the hedges. The spiders' webs had turned into diamond necklaces on the bushes by the gate.

It was the perfect morning for a magical adventure, Molly thought to herself, as she blew on her fingers. It would be nice if it warmed up a bit, that was all.

Walking slowly through the mist towards her came a beautiful silver-white creature. It was Silver. His horn was much clearer now – perhaps he could hide it, Molly wondered, if he needed to be in disguise. Maybe she'd only seen it on Saturday because he was upset. It was obvious that Silver wanted her to see it now.

"Hello, Molly," Silver said, out loud this time. His voice was low and musical.

"You came!" Molly said shyly. Silver was so beautiful, she was a little scared to talk to him.

Silver nodded. "When you put your

hand on me, back at the forge, I knew I could trust you. So last night, when the people didn't shut the door of my stable properly, I slipped out after dark, and came to find you. I need your help."

Molly nodded. "I'll try my best. You *are* a unicorn, aren't you? I can hardly believe you're real."

Silver laughed. "I am real. Touch me!" And he stepped closer, nuzzling against Molly's hand.

Molly gently stroked his neck. Such a delicious feeling of warmth ran through her, it sparkled all the way to her fingertips.

"See? You're not imagining me." Silver tossed his mane.

"I've only ever heard of unicorns in fairy tales. Are they everywhere, and I just didn't realize?" Molly was thinking of Bella and Treacle. Were they really unicorns in disguise too?

"No, we're very rare. People hardly ever see us now, it's too dangerous. I live in a hidden wood, deep in the mountains. There's a unicorn herd there – a blessing of unicorns, it's called, when there are lots of us – but I wanted to explore. I went wandering, and I was caught. Oh, they didn't know what I was, they just thought I was a pretty pony, with no owner around, and that they'd sell me on."

"Couldn't you stop them?" Molly asked. Silver's horn looked rather sharp. She would have thought he could fight off anyone who tried to steal him.

Silver sighed. "I was too surprised. And – and I suppose a little bit scared. And I didn't want them to see I was a unicorn. Then they put a metal bridle on me. I can't stand iron, it dulls my powers. That's why I couldn't let your grandfather shoe me, with those iron horseshoes."

"So what happened then?" Molly asked breathlessly.

"They sold me to that woman, Mrs James. She wanted me for her daughter to ride. Alice is a nice girl, a lot nicer than her mother. She seems lonely, they've only been living here a little while, I think, and she doesn't have many friends yet." Silver's eyes were troubled, as though he was worried about the girl.

"Alice! Oh, does she have curly hair? We've got a new girl in our class, she's called Alice."

Silver nodded. "Yes, dark hair, very curly. She's very kind, and brings me apples, and sugar, but she doesn't want to ride me. I think she must have had a fall once, she's scared to ride now, and her mother gets very cross with her about it. I think I was rather expensive..." He snorted, as though he thought this was quite silly. "She likes stroking me though, and she buys me packets of something called Polos. She shares them with me."

He sighed. "Delicious..."

Molly looked at him worriedly. "Alice doesn't talk that much at school. She's only been here a couple of weeks, but she's ever so quiet. I've said hello to her a few times, and chatted with her a bit, and she seems really friendly, but she doesn't say much. I think she's still getting used to us. I just wish ... well, I wish you'd belonged to somebody who wasn't so nice."

Silver shook his mane again, showering Molly with silvery sparkles. "I know.

She'll be sad that I've gone." His voice was very quiet. "And I will miss her, even though they kept me shut up, which was horrible." His eyelids fluttered closed for a second, and when they opened again, his eyes were black with fear. "I can't stay there, Molly. If I stay, they'll put those iron shoes on me, and I'll be a prisoner and I'll lose my magic. I have to be free!"

Chapter Four

The Spell in the Orchard

"Can you do magic as well, then?" Molly asked in surprise. Silver was so rare and special, and he could talk in her head, so she hadn't really expected that he could do other magic too.

Silver nodded. "All unicorns have magical powers, Molly." He nuzzled her cheek gently. "And you have too, haven't you? It isn't just that you can see me, and hear me talking, you can do magic spells. I'm sure I can feel it in you."

Molly blushed, and nodded. "I've only ever done one spell on my own," she explained. "That was bewitching some daisy petals." Molly explained about Snowdrop, the mischievous vanishing rabbit. "And I did spells with a witch's kitten called Sparkle, too, and with Star and Stella, the wish puppies."

Molly smiled dreamily to herself,

remembering the wonderful feeling of magic fizzing through her body as she helped with the spells. Then all at once she looked up, worriedly. "Silver, I've just had an awful thought. You need to hide! If you stay here, someone's bound to notice you, and send you back to Mrs James. I bet she'll call the police, and put signs up, all that sort of thing."

Silver nodded. "I know. I must go back home, but it's a long journey, and difficult. I need a little time to rest before I set off, just a few days to get strong again. Being shut away in that stable has left me weak."

Molly frowned. "I'd love it if you could stay here, but the orchard is so close to the house. My mum and dad and Kitty – that's my little sister – they all go past here every day. One of them would be bound to spot you. You can't turn invisible or anything like that, can you?" she added, thinking of Snowdrop the rabbit.

Silver snorted a horsy laugh. "No, I'm afraid not. But I do have an idea, and I think you might be able to help. Climb up on my back, Molly."

Molly hesitated. "Are you sure?" Somehow it felt very special to ride a unicorn, as though it was something that only princesses, or fairies, ought to be allowed to do.

Silver snorted again, and nudged her with his nose. "Of course, silly. I want you to. Besides, I need you to help me with the spell."

Molly smiled at him shyly. "I'd love to." She climbed up a couple more rungs of the gate, and carefully threw her leg over Silver's back. She'd ridden bareback once at the stables, but Silver was much more slender and graceful than dear old Whisky, who was like riding a table. She wriggled

experimentally to see how well she
could stay on, but Silver shook his mane,
and tossed his head. "That tickles! Don't
worry, Molly, I won't let you fall."

Molly patted his neck gently. "I don't
feel like I *could* fall," she admitted. It
was as though she and Silver had been
joined into one person. She could sense
the magic racing all round his body,

and now she was part of it too.

"Good." Silver set off at a walk round the orchard, looking carefully at the trees. "I shall know when I come to the right place," he muttered. "Ah! This — this is perfect." He was standing by Molly's favourite apple tree, a big old one which was easy to climb, and had the most delicious sweet, crunchy apples. "Hold on tight," Silver told her, looking back over his shoulder.

Molly leaned forward and hugged him tightly round the neck, and Silver started to walk slowly backwards around the tree, lowering his head so that his horn drew a magical circle in the dewy grass. The circle flared silver, glowing and sparkling in the sunlight, and Molly's fingers glittered as her magic joined the circle too.

When he had gone all the way round the tree, Silver stepped inside the circle and Molly slipped from his back. They looked at it delightedly. "That is *very* good," Silver told her with a little whinny of pleasure. "Your magic works beautifully with mine. Now, only we two will be able to enter this circle, and when we're in it, no one will be able to see us. I can hide here and rest for as long as I need."

Molly stared admiringly at the circle, and then she gasped. "Silver, look! The apples!"

Silver looked up into the tree where she was pointing. The last

few apples at the top of the tree were shining softly silver too.

"Aren't they beautiful?" Molly breathed softly, and Silver rubbed his head fondly against her shoulder. Molly patted his velvety nose. "Your magic is amazing, Silver. You're so clever. I never knew unicorns could do spells."

Silver looked pleased. "Well, mostly we're known for healing. Our horns can heal wounds, you know, or cure people who've been poisoned."

"Wow," Molly whispered. "That's really special."

Silver stared sadly over her shoulder, looking into the distance. "It is a wonderful gift," he agreed. "But we can hardly ever use it."

"Why not?" Molly frowned, puzzled. "Is it very difficult to do? I suppose it is. I should think it would wear you out, healing people."

Silver's head drooped. "No, it's hard, but not too hard. It's because once I cure someone, Molly, they know what I am. Oh, sometimes we can do it secretly. But that's very difficult."

"And once they know what you are..." Molly said thoughtfully.

"Once they know what I am, Molly, they want me to belong to them. So they can use my magic for themselves. Some people would even steal our horns."

"You mean, cut them off?" Molly gasped in horror.

Silver nodded, closing his eyes and shuddering at the idea.

"That's awful," Molly whispered. "Would it ... grow back?"

"Eventually. But it would be very

painful." Silver stared anxiously at his horn,
which meant he went rather cross-eyed.

Molly leaned against the gate, thinking
hard. "My dad is a vet, did you know
that? He heals animals, that's his job."

Silver shook his mane. "I didn't know.
He must be very special."

"Oh, he is!" Molly agreed. "I was
just thinking, though. I know he'd love
to have magical healing powers, but I
don't think he'd ever steal a unicorn

horn. In fact, I'm sure he wouldn't."

Silver sighed. "It's hard to know who to trust. I'm sure you're right about your father, but if he found a unicorn in his garden, what would he do?"

Molly looked doubtful. "I'm not sure. Maybe tell lots of other vets? I should think they'd all want to see you. They'd be amazed!"

"And would you trust every one of these other vets, and all the people they would tell?"

"Oh..." Molly shook her head slightly. "No. No, I suppose not. I see what you mean."

"I can only tell people that I can trust to keep my secret," Silver told her gently.

"I won't tell *anyone*!" Molly promised. It was a little frightening to have such an important secret. Then she sighed.

"What is it? Are you wishing you hadn't found me?" Silver asked anxiously.

"Oh, no!" Molly assured him. "I just wish that you *could* use your healing powers here, that's all. My dad has a cat at the surgery at the moment, she was hit by a car, and she's very ill. He did a big operation on her on Saturday, the morning I met you at Grandad's forge, but she's not doing very well..."

Silver's ears pricked forward interestedly. "I could try to help. If the cat doesn't get better, perhaps we could do it without your father knowing. I've never tried to heal a cat, but I'm sure I could."

Molly flung her arms around the unicorn's neck. It felt like hugging any other pony, except for the wonderful fizzing, sparkling sensation that rushed through her as she buried her face in his mane, and whispered, "Oh, thank you, Silver!"

Chapter Five

Alice's Story

Molly stayed hugging Silver for what seemed like ages. The wonderful magic in his mane made her feel so happy and strong.

"My dad would be so pleased if we could help Sasha," she whispered hopefully. Then she gasped and looked up. "My dad! Oh, Silver, what time is it? We've been here ages. Mum and Dad will be getting up soon, and they'll wonder where I am. I'd better go. Will you be all right here on your own?"

Silver nodded. "Of course you must go. But you will visit me later, won't you?" he asked wistfully.

"As soon as I get back from school," Molly promised. She gave him a quick kiss on the nose, and raced back to the gate, scrambling over and making a dash for the house. "Oh no," she muttered, as she saw her dad sitting at the kitchen table. She'd hoped she'd be able to get in before her parents noticed she was gone. Molly shut the back door behind with a soft click, and waited for her dad to ask her where on earth she'd been.

He didn't. He took a sip of his coffee, and smiled sadly at her. "Hi Molly," he murmured.

Molly stared at him. Not even one

question about why she was outside? Molly looked at the kitchen clock. It was only six-thirty. Well, that was good, because Mum probably hadn't tried to wake her up yet. But why was Dad so dopey? And why was he in the kitchen at half-past six in the morning? Usually he liked his sleep.

"Is everything OK, Dad?" Molly asked worriedly.

Her dad shook his head. "I just went to

check on Sasha, the hit-and-run cat. She's not doing well, Molly. I'm thinking we might lose her. It's just such a shame."

"Oh, Dad..." Molly breathed.

"She's such a friendly little thing. I've had her in the surgery for vaccinations and everyday stuff. And her owners – two little girls, Molly, they're going to be devastated." Dad stared across the room, frowning. "I've tried everything, Molly. I'm just not sure what else I can do..."

Molly caught her breath. Maybe there wasn't much else Dad could do for Sasha, but there *was* something she could do. If only she could get Silver into the surgery...

Molly was very silent on the walk to school, as she tried to work out some way of getting Sasha and Silver together.

She waved goodbye to Mum and Kitty
at the gates to the nursery, and walked
slowly on to the school entrance, not
bothering to run in after her friends like
she usually would. As she turned into the
gates, a car drew up. Molly ducked behind
the gatepost when she saw Mrs James get
out. She really didn't want Silver's owner
to see her right now! She just couldn't
like her – she wasn't sure how Mrs James

had managed to have a daughter as nice as Alice.

Mrs James seemed just as cross as she had on Saturday. "Hurry up, Alice! Don't forget your recorder!"

Alice obediently hustled herself out of the car, laden with bags and her coat.

"I'm going off to the police station now, to tell them about the pony. Who knows if we'll ever hear anything..." Mrs James muttered.

Alice nodded. "Bye Mum," she called quietly, as Mrs James got into the car, and she waved her recorder. Alice watched the car go off round the corner, and sighed. Then she turned and looked at the playground, full of people chatting, or racing about, and she sighed again, and walked very slowly in. She sat down on one of the benches, and looked wistfully at a group of girls from their class talking.

Molly was very tempted to go and talk to her — she really wanted to know what Alice thought of Silver, whether she had any idea what he really was — but the bell went, and they had to hurry into school.

But at lunch time, Molly sat down nervously next to Alice. She was on that same bench again. Alice gave her a shy

smile, and Molly smiled back. She took a deep breath. Alice had seemed nice when she'd spoken to her a couple of times before, but Molly was still a little nervous.

"I was walking past you this morning, and I'm really sorry, but I couldn't help hearing your mum say she was going to the police about your pony. Is he all right?"

Alice shook her head sadly. "I don't know. He's gone."

"Oh no – do you think he's been stolen?" Molly asked, crossing her fingers under her skirt and feeling guilty. "That's awful. You must be really upset."

Alice looked thoughtfully at Molly, then lowered her voice to a whisper. "I let him go."

"What?" Molly squeaked. She certainly hadn't been expecting that.

"I left the bolt on the stable door undone. I stuck a piece of paper in the door, so it looked closed." Alice stared at her fingers.

"*Why?*" Molly asked her disbelievingly.

Alice looked up at her. "He wasn't happy," she murmured. "I don't like riding any more and I don't know an awful lot about ponies, but even I could see that.

Maybe I could tell because I'm not very happy either," she added quietly. "He just kept staring out of the stable door, looking out across the field to the woods, as though he was desperate to get away. It looked like he wanted to go home. I know how he felt. So I let him go."

Alice blinked. "But I wish I hadn't. He might not have been able to find his way back there. What if he's been hurt on the road somewhere?" She sniffed. "And I really miss him. He was so lovely. Even though I didn't want to ride him, I loved brushing him, and stroking his mane."

She smiled a shy smile at Molly. "He had the most gorgeous mane, you wouldn't believe. Just stroking it made me feel all sparkly and happy. You probably think I'm being stupid," she said defensively.

Molly shook her head. "No, I believe you," she said earnestly. "I really do. Some animals are like that." It was all she could say without giving away too much of the truth, but it seemed to help Alice.

"Thanks," she murmured, blowing her nose. "I'm glad I told you. You won't tell anyone else, will you?" she asked, suddenly anxious.

Molly shook her head. She *was* planning to tell someone what Alice had said, but she didn't think Alice would mind...

Molly crept out of the house while Mum was reading a story to Kitty that afternoon after school. Mum probably thought she was doing her homework, but this was a lot more important. She raced over to the orchard, and clambered over the gate.

Silver looked up anxiously as he heard her running across the grass. When he saw it was Molly, he gave a delighted whinny.

Molly stepped into the enchanted circle, shivering a little as the magic sparkled over her from top to toe. She hugged Silver, and he breathed sweet horsy breath down her neck.

Molly giggled. Then she said thoughtfully, "You know, Silver, I think Alice could feel your magic too."

Silver looked up eagerly. "You saw her? How is she? Was she missing me? I worry about her, she seemed so lonely."

Molly nodded. "*Very* lonely. She's really worried about you too. I think you were her only friend, Silver. And she still let you go."

Silver drew in a sharp breath. "You mean – *she* left the stable unbolted?"

"On purpose. She said you kept staring out at the woods like you were desperate to go home. And she knew how you felt, so she let you go." Molly's voice shook a little. It had been so brave of Alice.

Silver looked out across the orchard, his dark blue eyes troubled. "I've been thinking about this all day," he said at last. "We have to tell Alice where I am. We've got to trust her. She cared enough to give me my freedom. She deserves to know I'm safe."

Chapter Six

The Magic Apples

"I've been worrying about something else too," Silver told Molly, his tail flicking from side to side. "I can feel a sick creature nearby. Very sick, Molly. Whoever it is — I don't think they have much time left. But I'm sure I could help." His tail twitched anxiously, faster and faster, and Molly stroked his neck soothingly.

"I think it's Sasha you can feel," she explained. "The cat I told you about before. My dad says she's really sick, and he's worried he might lose her." She leaned her head against Silver's neck. "I just don't see how I can get you close enough to Sasha to heal her," she said, tearing a leaf into tiny pieces crossly. "I can't bring her out here, I'd never get her out without someone seeing us, and she's just too sick, anyway. Oh, what are we going to do? We can't just let her fade away!"

Molly stared up into the tree, blinking back tears. Shimmering high above her, the silver apples floated against the blue sky. Molly nibbled her lip thoughtfully. "Silver?" she asked at last. "Why did the apples change colour? After we made the magic circle, I mean?"

Silver looked up too. "I should think that some of our magic went into the ground, and up through the tree roots to the apples," he answered, not really paying attention. Then his furry ears pricked forward with sudden understanding. "Our magic is in the apples... Molly!"

"Do you think it will work?" Molly asked eagerly.

"Let's try! Climb up on my back, then you should be able to reach one." Silver moved as close as he could towards the tree, so that Molly could clamber up. Standing on tiptoe on his back, gripping on to the trunk, Molly stretched up into the tree, her fingertips just touching an apple. Its skin was smooth and silky, and it pulsed with magic as her fingers brushed against it.

"I shall rear a little," Silver warned her. "Hold tight. You should be able to reach – now!" Effortlessly he lifted his front hooves from the ground, and Molly gasped and grabbed the apple, sliding down on to Silver's back with a rustle of leaves.

"Are you all right?" Silver asked, nosing round at her anxiously.

"I think so!" Molly told him. Luckily she had her thick jacket on which had protected her. She gazed at the apple. It *looked* magical. It was still apple-coloured, but somehow it was silver as well. Not a cold, metallic silver, but a rich soft glowing colour. It smelled gorgeous too. Cats didn't normally like apples, but she was sure that even a cat would try this one.

"Hurry, Molly," Silver told her anxiously. "Go and try!"

Molly nodded, and slipped down from his back. She hurried over to the surgery. Luckily no one was in reception, and she crept quietly into the ward area.

Sasha was lying on her side in one of the cages. She was hardly even breathing, and one of her eyes was half open, and looked dull and grey. Molly gulped. Could anything save her? She had to try. She dug a tiny piece of apple out with her fingernail, and poked it through the wire. The apple was full of silvery, sweet-smelling juice. It dripped from Molly's finger on to Sasha's bluish mouth.

Nothing happened.

Then, very slowly, Sasha's tongue moved to lick the apple juice from the corner of her mouth.

Molly hurriedly pushed the rest of the

tiny piece of apple between her teeth, and Sasha's eyelids fluttered.

It was working!

After watching Sasha for a few more moments, Molly sneaked quietly out of the surgery again. She was intending to go back to the orchard to tell Silver that she thought the apple had started to work.

But when she came round the corner of the surgery, she discovered that there was no need to go to the orchard. Silver was already there. With Grandad.

Molly gulped.

I wanted to see if it had worked! Silver said anxiously in her head. *I was watching through the window. I think it will cure her, but we'll have to give it time. And ... I'm afraid we may have a small problem...*

Molly gazed speechlessly at them, thinking that actually Grandad looked to her like rather a big problem.

"Molly, this is Mrs James's pony, isn't it?" Grandad asked, sounding rather puzzled.

"Um, yes..." Molly admitted.

NO! Silver shouted silently, and Molly winced. That hurt.

"I mean, no... He was kidnapped..." Molly muttered, trying to think of a way to explain that didn't involve unicorns.

"But Ellie at the riding school told me that Mrs James has reported him to the police as stolen! Has he been here all the time?" Grandad asked worriedly.

At this point, Silver took two steps closer to Grandad, and butted his head into Grandad's shoulder, obviously asking to be given some attention. Grandad stroked his mane absent-mindedly. "Yes, you're very lovely," he murmured. "But Molly, we need to sort this out..." Grandad blinked, and then shook his head. "What was I saying?"

Molly smiled to herself as she saw the silver sparkles rising out of Silver's mane, and wafting round Grandad. Silver had bewitched him, so that Grandad had forgotten that this was a stolen pony, and even that Molly shouldn't have a pony in the yard at all!

"I still think there's something very odd about this pony," Grandad said

thoughtfully, looking at Silver's forehead.
"Something I can't quite put my finger
on. . ."

Silver gazed at him innocently, trying to
look ever so normal, and spoke in Molly's
mind. *Your grandfather can almost see I'm a
unicorn, Molly. He isn't quite as magical as
you, but nearly. I think you could trust him*

to help you, if you should ever need to.

Molly nodded. "I'm going to take Silver back now," she said hesitantly, not sure how Grandad would react.

"Yes, yes, of course," Grandad murmured, still staring unseeingly at Silver's horn. "I hope I'll see him again, he's a beautiful creature." And he turned, and wandered away round the front of the surgery.

"Wow! Your magic is really strong!" Molly told Silver admiringly. "That was amazing – and I'm sure Sasha is starting to get better, did you see her? She had her eyes open, just for a minute, and then she fell asleep again, but it was different sleep. Her breathing was stronger, and I really think her fur was glossier too. We'll just have to wait and see."

Silver pawed the ground shyly. "I'm glad it worked. And I'm sorry I came out of the circle – I just wanted to see." Then he sighed. "Now all we need to do is help Alice. But I think that could be the hardest job of all."

Molly waited for Alice at the gate the next morning – she was hoping that if she could persuade her to come to tea, Alice could ask her mother right then. Molly had already asked Mum, who thought it was a lovely idea, especially when Alice didn't know many people yet. She promised that she would be sure to have enough tea in case Alice was able to come.

As soon as Alice's car pulled up, Molly ran over to her, and smiled politely at Mrs James. Mrs James frowned slightly –

she obviously remembered who Molly was, but she looked pleased when Molly invited Alice round. Molly looked hopefully at Alice. *Please say yes!* she told her silently, wishing she could really talk in people's minds, like Silver could.

"Oh!" Alice sounded delighted. "Oh, yes, please!" And she beamed at Molly, looking less shy than Molly had ever seen her. They went on into school together, chatting happily about how awful their science homework was.

After school, Alice walked back home with Molly and Mum and Kitty. Mum was really happy, and told them all that the poor cat in the surgery had started to get better. Molly smiled to herself. Silver had done it! And she had helped him!

Mum got them all some raisins to

nibble on while they were waiting for tea,
and persuaded Kitty to help her cook.
She gave Molly and Alice a smiling look,
which meant that she knew they didn't
want Kitty hanging around, and suggested
that Molly showed Alice round outside.
Molly agreed delightedly – she'd been
wondering how they'd get out to see
Silver without Kitty.

"Come and see the orchard," she suggested to Alice. "There's some really good trees to climb."

They leaned on the orchard gate together, Alice telling Molly about her old house. Molly wasn't really listening. She was peering through the trees, hoping that Silver would hear them. *Silver, Alice is here!* she called to him. *Come out!*

Silver came stepping silently through the trees. Molly thought he looked anxious, as though he was worried how Alice might react to seeing him. He needn't have been. Alice gasped, then scrambled over the gate so fast she fell, though she didn't seem to care about her scraped knees. She raced across the grass to Silver, and hugged him, burying her face in his mane, while he nuzzled at her delightedly.

Molly followed her slowly, wanting to give them some time alone together. As she came closer, Alice looked up. "You found him!" she said, her eyes shining.

Molly nodded. "He turned up here on Monday. That's why I asked you about him at school. I'm sorry, I didn't know who he belonged to." It was *almost* true.

I don't belong to anyone! Silver tossed his head, and his voice in Molly's mind was stern.

Alice looked up at him, blinking. She looked confused, and Molly wondered how much she could see.

"I don't think he's mine, Molly," she said hesitantly. "I think he's got somewhere else to go. I wish he'd stay with me, I've missed him so much, but I want him to be happy. I'm just pleased to know he's safe." She sighed. "I – I almost think I could ride him. I fell off at my riding school last year, and I broke my leg, really badly. Mum bought me Silver to try and persuade me to ride again, but I didn't want to. He's so gentle though. I'm sure he wouldn't let me fall. . ." She gazed at Silver lovingly.

Then she gulped, and turned bravely to Molly. "Maybe if he stays here, could I come and visit him sometimes? This is such a beautiful place, I can see why he'd want to stay. It's almost magical, isn't it?" She looked round at the trees, their leaves turning golden in the autumn sun.

"I think he has to go," Molly said sadly. "He doesn't really belong here."

I could stay, Silver told her silently, and Molly looked up at him in surprise. *I do like it, being with people. It's interesting. And she needs me. If she promises never to put iron shoes on me, I'll stay.*

Molly looked thoughtfully at Alice. How was she going to explain that? Alice was still leaning lovingly against Silver's shoulder, her fingers twisted in his mane. Molly gave Silver a meaningful look, and

he snorted in agreement. A silver glow
wrapped softly around Alice, making
her sigh happily, her eyelashes fluttering
against her cheeks. She nodded, as if she
understood something very important.

"Could your grandad make silver
horseshoes?" she murmured to Molly.
Molly smiled. "I'm sure he could."

If he does, Silver said happily, *I'll still be a unicorn, but I'll be Alice's unicorn, and she'll be able to ride me.*

Molly stroked his velvety nose, and sighed. It was the happiest ending she could have wished for.

One day soon, she was sure, she would have her own pet to love, just as much as Alice loved Silver.

Read more about Molly's magical adventures!

She can talk to animals!

Molly's Magic

The Witch's Kitten

HOLLY WEBB

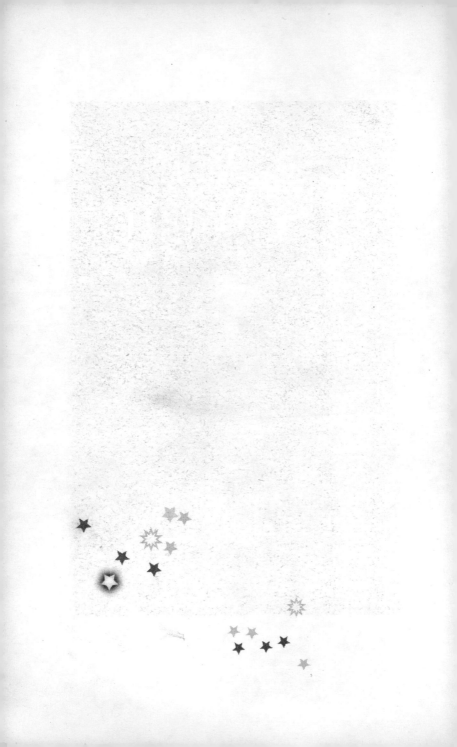

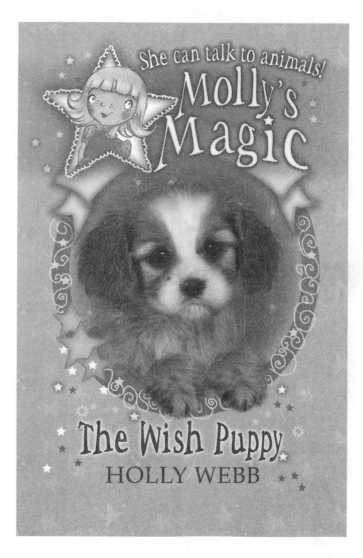

She can talk to animals!

Molly's Magic

The Wish Puppy

HOLLY WEBB

★ She can talk to animals! ★

Molly's Magic

The Invisible Bunny

HOLLY WEBB

If you liked this book, try these!

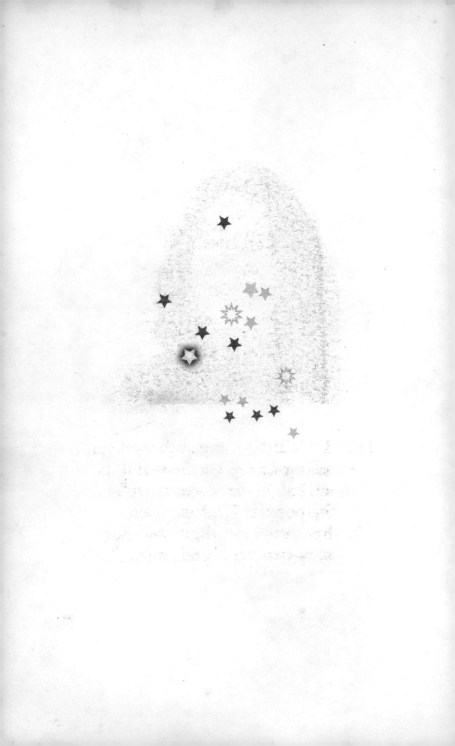

HOLLY WEBB is the author of the
bestselling *Lost in the Snow* and its
sequel, *Lost in the Storm*, as well as
the popular Triplets series.
She has always loved cats and now
owns two very spoilt ones.

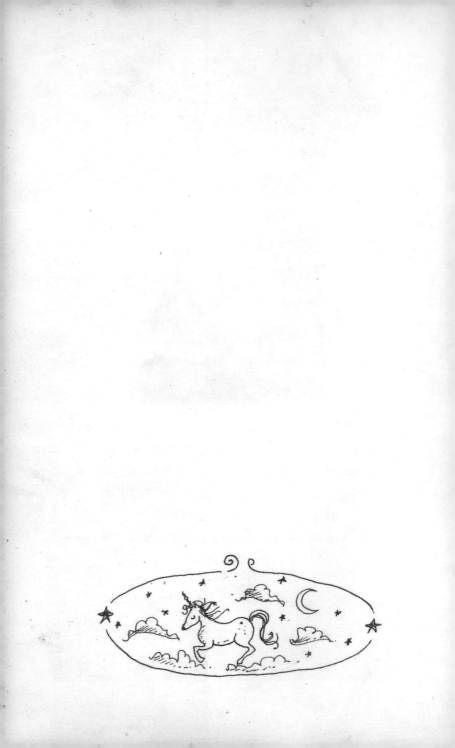